Ice Harbor Mittens

by Robin Hansen

Illustrated by Jamie Hogan

Text copyright © 2010 by Robin Hansen

Illustrations copyright © 2010 by Jamie Hogan

All rights reserved

ISBN 978-0-89272-905-0

Design by Rich Eastman

Printed in China

5   4   3   2   1

BOOKS·MAGAZINE·ONLINE
www.downeast.com

Distributed to the trade by National Book Network

Library of Congress Cataloging-in-Publication Data Available on Request

For Finn, Ellis, and Anne, island inspirations all
—J.H.

For Maine fishing kids and the good women who knit for their communities
—R.H.

"If you're going to be sternman on Sam Eldredge's boat this winter, you're going to need a pair of compass mittens," Aunt Agnes told Josiah when she stopped by for a load of crab to pick.

Josie grinned proudly. If he was getting his own pair of compass mittens, he must be getting to be a man. All the men who worked on boats in Ice Harbor had compass mittens knitted by Aunt Agnes. The design on the mittens was little wheels laid side by side, with lines pointing north and south and east and west.

Aunt Agnes put her hand flat against Josie's to see how long his fingers were. They were the same length, although Josie was eleven and Aunt Agnes was probably as old as the rock her house stood on. She took his hand in hers to see how fat it was, too. Josie was a little scared when she did that, with her hand as dry and skinny as an osprey's claw.

The day the mittens were ready, Josie went to Aunt Agnes's little house overlooking the bay. He put on the mittens, and his hopes slid out the scuppers into the bay. "They're too big," he whispered, afraid she would take them back, and he wouldn't be able to work on Sam's boat when it turned cold.

Aunt Agnes's dark eyes crinkled. "They'll shrink up in the salt water and fish gore. If they're still too big next Sunday, you bring them back, and I'll make you a smaller pair."

The next morning, when Josie met his older cousin Sam walking down to the wharf, he waved at him with one of the new mittens.

"Hmph," Sam said. "Got yourself a pair of Aunt Agnes's old-time compass mittens, do you? Look what I got." He held up his hands. Sam's mittens had a pattern of little red triangles all over. They fit his hands perfectly.

"Woman over to Woolwich made them for me. I paid her five dollars," Sam said. "They've got red on them, so's you can find them easy. And the sawteeth all point into the center. Like the way you want to go."

Josie wished he had a pair like Sam's, instead of a pair of too-big, old-fashioned, black-and-white compass mittens. Aunt Agnes's mittens had only cost a quarter.

Sam showed him how to dunk the compass mittens in the cooling water from *Lily Mae*'s engine and to wring them half dry before putting them on. "Then clap your hands around your body like this to get your blood flowing." He slapped himself on the back of his shoulders and danced around a little. "That way, your hands'll stay warm when they get wet."

That day while Josie worked the mittens rubbed on the traps and on the hauling lines. And they warmed up on the engine at lunch. When Josie took them off in the afternoon, they didn't look new anymore. They looked like the mittens men wore on boats, kind of rubbed and fuzzed and matted. They were even a dite smaller, but they didn't have bright red sawteeth.

When they sold their lobsters that day, Josie saw that some of the other older boys had new sawtooth mittens, too, and were showing them off.

Josie went to Aunt Agnes's house up on the rock. She gave him a cup of warm cocoa and teased him a little. "Are your mittens still too big?"

The cocoa felt good after being out in the cold all day. "A little. But they're working at shrinking."

"Are they too cold? You work a hole in them already?" Aunt Agnes asked, smiling.

Josie didn't know what to say. "No. They're warm. But, Aunt—"

"Yes? But what?"

"I wondered—" Josie didn't want to say it, but he did want red and gray sawtooth mittens that fit his hands, and he couldn't go to Woolwich, and he didn't have five dollars. "I wondered if you could make me mittens with little red triangles instead. Sawtooth mittens." There. He had said it.

Aunt Agnes's osprey-sharp eyes seemed to shrink him into a little kid. He couldn't even mention the quarter he had in his pocket to pay for the new mittens. "Like Sam Eldredge's," he added in a tiny voice.

"Sawtooth, is it?" She asked finally in a quiet, hard voice that was worse than Mom's when she was angry. "Sawtooth!" she said again, and her anger was like a cold wind in the warm little house. "Sawtooth is for farm boys. You're a fishing boy, about to be a fisher*man*, Josie Eldredge. You go get yourself sawtooth mittens from Amelia Perkins over to Woolwich if you want, but don't you trust them like compass mittens that shrink and mold to your hands, with lines that point north and south and east and west."

Josie felt hot all over and was glad when Aunt Agnes told him to get on home.

When he got home, Josie said to his mom, "That mean old Aunt Agnes won't make me a pair of sawtooth mittens."

"She already made you compass mittens, didn't she?" His mom asked.

Josie stuck out his lower lip.

"Didn't she? With lines that point north and south and east and west?"

"But — "

"Did you thank her for them?"

He hadn't. He had never said thank you for his new mittens. "I paid her a quarter," he said.

"You didn't thank her?" his mom asked again. "I'll make her a lobster stew tomorrow while you're out with Sam. That's her favorite. You take it to her tomorrow afternoon, and you say thank you."

"Okay. But—"

"No buts, mister," his mom said. "She made those mittens for you because you're an Ice Harbor boy commencing to fish. Not for your little quarter. Ice Harbor men wear compass mittens. To bring them home safe. They're our good luck."

Josie thought that was stupid, but he didn't dare say so.

The next morning when Sam and Josie walked down to the wharf, a fog bank lay offshore like a gray whale lolling on top of the water.

"It'll burn off," Sam said to Ed Prower, who was mending net at the wharf.

"I don't mind you should head out 'til then," Ed Prower said.

"We'll be okay," Sam said. "I was born at night, but not last night."

"Maybe. How much you going to catch, since you know everything?" Ed Prower snapped back. "You oughtn't to head out 'til it burns off." Josie knew what he meant was, "I don't want to have to come out after you."

Sam and Josie climbed into the dory and loaded in the herring. Josie stood in the stern and sculled with one long oar. It was hard, but he leaned into it to show Sam and Ed Prower that he could do it. Sam nodded and smiled and pretended he didn't see Ed Prower scowling after them.

The *Lily Mae* sat out in the harbor on a mooring. From the wharf, Josie saw only her shape in the fog, but by the time they got to her, she was clear enough. Josie looked back at the wharf and saw only fog.

But Sam knew when to go out and when not to. Still, it was a little scary not being able to see the wharf or the shoreline. As he climbed on board, Josie saw his hands and the fuzzy compass mittens. "Luck," Mom had said. To bring them home safe.

He could hear gulls over to the fish processing plant, and he could hear the generator chugging by the store, and he could hear Ed Prower's dragger bang lightly against the pilings in the rising tide. It was like being in bed at night. You couldn't see anything, but you could tell where everything was.

They chugged out, and Josie filled bait bags with chopped herring, then got the banding elastics out and the jig to fit them on the lobsters' claws. The crisp, cold air blowing back along the deck took most of the old fish smell overboard.

Sam slowed, and the hydraulic winch screamed as he hauled in a trap, opened it, and tossed fish and too-small lobsters back. He hooked his gauge over the carapace of one lobster and then another, and put them, flopping and wiggling, on the table for Josie to band.

Another burst of engine and a rooster-tail wake, another trap, one lobster, four crabs. Another. Then another. Josie was keeping up okay when Sam slowed *Lily Mae*.

Josie looked up. Sam was peering side to side into the fog.

"Should be one right here. Don't know where it's got to," Sam said thoughtfully. He gunned the engine and *Lily Mae* made large loops in the water. Looking out from the boat was like trying to see out of a milk jug. There was nothing but white.

"Fog's thickened instead of burning off," Sam said. "Getting colder, too."

Something banged and scraped the bottom of the boat, and they lurched and had to catch the rail to stay on their feet. "Drat!" Sam said. "We're too close in." Josie listened, and heard water clucking on stone to the starboard. Sam swung the wheel and headed away from the sound.

They hadn't gone too far when Sam slowed. The fog was still thick, but the sound of water on rocks was behind them. "Looks like I should've listened to old Ed," he said. Josie felt an uneasy tickle crawl around the back of his neck.

"Crack out a sandwich, would you?" Sam said sharply and leaned back against the deck housing as if he wasn't worried at all.

Josie reached into the dinner pail and pulled out a lobster sandwich. They split it and ate. Josie thought it was a big mouthful of food he didn't want just then. Sam poured a cup of coffee into the thermos lid and handed it to him.

Josie looked at it. "I'm a kid."

"Hey, this one time." Sam pushed it at him. "Tastes awful, but it warms you through."

Josie sipped at the coffee, thick with milk and sugar. It tasted like coffee ice cream—not his favorite, but awful good hot. It wet down the glob of lobster sandwich some, and the cup warmed through his wet mittens.

"Gotta think," Sam said, taking another bite of sandwich.

"Are we lost?" Josie asked.

"Kind of. But I'll sort it out."

"Can't we use a compass to get home?"

"Could," Sam answered. "If we had one. Never needed one before."

An osprey chirped overhead, wheeling above them in the fog. Josie thought the ospreys had already flown south, and for no good reason he thought of Aunt Agnes.

Compass mittens, to bring them home safe.

He looked over at Sam's sawtooth mittens. They looked fuzzed and matted like his compass mittens. But they had shrunk, too, and now didn't even cover Sam's wrists.

He looked at his own mittens. They had shrunk to fit and molded perfectly to his hands. Compass mittens with lines that pointed north and south and east and west.

Then a movement on the mittens caught his eye. A set of lines was shining, in one direction. He moved his hands cattycorner and the shiny part shifted to the diagonals.

"Sam," he said. "Look at my mittens."

"Yeah, I know. Aunt Agnes made them for you, and all that. Shut up, okay?"

"No, for real. Check them out." He put his hands out toward Sam, and the shiny part moved again, as if each little fiber of the wool was a skinny little diode. "They're pointing. That way. See the light?"

Sam looked and looked, then shook his head. "For real," he said softly. "I'd heard, but I thought it was just tales."

"What's it mean? Are we supposed to go that way?"

"Don't know. Might mean that." He wiggled one of Josie's hands side to side and the shine of them flickered around some more.

Off the stern, Josie heard the water clucking on the rocks again. He bit his lip to forget about crying, then said, "A compass points north."

"Might mean north." Sam agreed, looking at him. "So, where are we?" he asked, staring out into the fog.

Josie said, "I heard an osprey just now."

Sam nodded. "Me, too. And that osprey hangs around Bateman Ledge. In summer, anyhow. But the tide is full, and we wouldn't run onto that, so that ledge we nearly fetched up on is probably the shoreline of Sabino. That would make that—" he pointed toward the stern of the boat "—east. Let's see your compass mittens again."

Josie held them out, pointing the tips toward where they'd come from. The shine in them was on the sideways lines.

"Okay, point them that way." He turned Josie's mittens to the left, and the lights lined up lengthwise on the mittens. "It's north. They're telling us north." He laughed, and gunned the engine. "And we need to go south to get home. Without running onto Bateman Ledge or the Sabino shore."

"You go up on the bow, sternman," Sam told him, "and hold on. Keep a listen and a lookout for rocks, in case we're too close in. The shore bulges out near here. Leave me one of them compass mittens. You take one of mine. They're too small for me anyways."

The osprey chirped again overhead as they began carefully chugging into blind fog.

Josie perched in the bow, trying to make his eyes cut through the fog, through the green-black water below.

He heard a chainsaw not far away. To the east, someone was cutting trees at Sabino. A dog barked. A Sabino dog. He glanced at his compass mitten. It looked like an ordinary mitten again, rubbed and matted and molded to his hand. Then it flickered just a dite and went out. He shivered in his rain gear and stared into the fog.

Gong, gong! It was the bell buoy off Bear Island, to the south. They were going the right way. It seemed a long time with no other sound but the buoy and the engine. Then Josie heard the gulls at the fish processing plant and the chug of the generator at the Ice Harbor Store.

He looked back. Sam was grinning like a dolphin and flicked him a little wave with Josie's mitten.

Josie would go thank Aunt Agnes right off. Soon's he got his other mitten back.